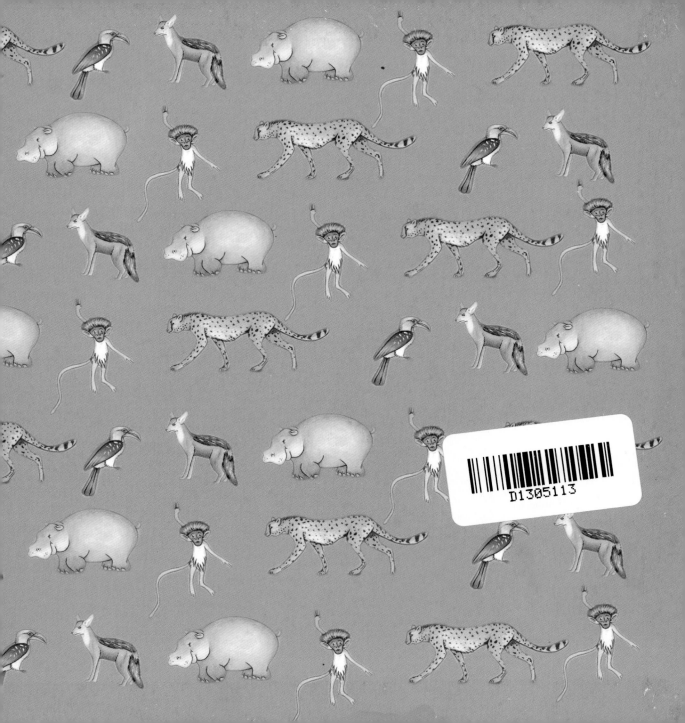

ISBN 0 86037 344 4

MUSLIM CHILDREN'S LIBRARY

HILMY THE HIPPO SERIES

HILMY THE HIPPO
Learns not to Lie

Author *Rae Norridge*
Illustrator *Leigh Norridge Marucchi*
Designer *Nasir Cadir*
Co-ordinator *Anwar Cara*

Published by
The Islamic Foundation
Markfield Conference Centre
Ratby Lane, Markfield
Leicester LE67 9SY
United Kingdom
T (01530) 244 944
F (01530) 244 946
E i.foundation@islamic-foundation.org.uk
    publications@islamic-foundation.com

Quran House, PO Box 30611, Nairobi, Kenya

PMB 3193, Kano, Nigeria

British Library Cataloguing in Publication Data

Norridge, Rae
    Hilmy the hippo learns not to lie
    1. Hilmy the Hippo (Fictitious character) - Pictorial works
    - Juvenile fiction 2. Truthfulness and falsehood - Pictorial
    works - Juvenile fiction 3. Children's stories - Pictorial
    works
    I. Title II. Marucchi, Leigh Norridge
    823.9'2 [J]

ISBN 0860373444

HILMY THE HIPPO

Rae Norridge

Learns not to Lie

Illustrated by *Leigh Norridge Marucchi*

THE ISLAMIC FOUNDATION

One bright, sunny morning Hilmy splashed about in his waterhole. He was feeling very lonely and decided it would be nice if he could make some new friends. So he climbed out of the water, said goodbye to the blue dragonfly, and set out in search of friendship.

He had not walked very far when he met another young hippo.

"*As-Salamu 'Alaykum,*" called Hilmy. "What is your name?"
"*Wa 'Alaykum as-Salam,*" replied the young hippo. "My name is Mina, and I live along the banks of the nearby river. What's your name?"

"My name is Hilmy." He was very happy to find another hippo so similar to himself.

"Will you be my friend?" asked Hilmy.
"Yes, of course I will be your friend Hilmy," replied Mina.
"I have lots and lots of friends."

4

Hilmy felt rather jealous that someone should have so many friends. "I am a special hippo," said Hilmy, trying his utmost to impress Mina. "I can fly. All my friends call me Hilmy the flying hippo."

"Well Hilmy," said Mina raising her eyebrows in surprise, "tomorrow, *Insha' Allah*, you can fly over to the river where I live and you can meet all my friends. *Fi Amanillah*, Hilmy, I will see you tomorrow."

5

Hilmy was very happy and continued on his way. He was very pleased with himself as he knew his new friend, Mina, was very impressed with him.

From a nearby bush Hilmy heard a voice calling. It was Bill Hornbill. Bill Hornbill was a bird renowned for his cheekiness. "*As-Salamu 'Alaykum*, Hilmy," squawked Bill. "I hear you are looking for new friends."

"*Wa 'Alaykum as-Salam,*" replied Hilmy. "Yes, I want many friends, I want to be the most popular hippo in the land. After all I am a special hippo."

"What makes you a special hippo, Hilmy?" asked the bird.

Hilmy had to think very quickly, he had to bear in mind that Bill Hornbill was a bird and Bill Hornbill could fly.

"Well," replied Hilmy, "I can run very fast. In fact, I can run faster than the cheetah."

"Really," said Bill Hornbill with some surprise. "That is very fast indeed. The cheetah is the fastest animal on earth."

Hilmy went on his way. He was very pleased with himself, as he was quite sure that Bill Hornbill was very impressed.

9

That evening as the sun was setting, and the sky had turned a glowing red, a jackal came down to Hilmy's waterhole to drink.

"*As-Salamu 'Alaykum,* Hilmy," called the jackal. "I hear you are looking for new friends. I will be your friend."

"*Wa 'Alaykum as-Salam*, Jackal," replied Hilmy. "That would be very nice, I would love to have you as my friend."

"I hear you can fly Hilmy," said the jackal. "That is really something to be proud of. And I hear from Bill Hornbill that you can run faster than the cheetah. You are truly an amazing hippo, Hilmy."

11

Hilmy puffed out his chest proudly and said, "*Subhan Allah,* that is not all. I can also climb and scamper up trees quicker than any baboon. I can run up a sheer cliff face, better than any rock-rabbit."

"I am impressed, Hilmy," said the jackal. "I would really like to have such a clever friend."

The jackal finished drinking and went on his way. Hilmy lay down on the sand beside his waterhole. *Masha' Allah*, he said to himself; I am very happy, I am making many new friends.

The following day Hilmy set out for the river where Mina,
the young hippo, lived. When he reached the river he saw
that many animals had gathered along the bank.

Hilmy saw Bill Hornbill and asked the bird what was happening. "There is a young monkey stuck up a tree, and no one is able to help him," said Bill Hornbill. "Animals from far and wide have gathered to help, but no one has been able to. Soon, *Insha' Allah*, someone will arrive who can rescue him."

At that moment Hilmy heard Mina calling him. Hilmy pushed his way through the crowd to where Mina stood.

"Hilmy," she said gratefully, "I am so pleased you are here. You can fly. Fly up and rescue the poor little monkey from the tree."

"Well," replied Hilmy feeling very uncomfortable, "I would do just that. But I am afraid if I lift him out of the branches the little monkey might fall, causing him much injury."

"Well, Hilmy," squawked Bill Hornbill, "since you can run very fast, run and find the giraffe. He is tall enough to rescue the young monkey."

"Even though I can run very fast," replied Hilmy, "I have no idea where the giraffe can be found. I would be running around all day. Surely there must be a better way."

17

At that moment the jackal came and stood beside Hilmy. "You can climb up the tree and rescue the poor little monkey, Hilmy. You said you could climb trees better than any baboon."

"That is what I said, Jackal. But look at those branches, look how thin they are. The branches will simply break, and the little monkey will fall to the ground. It will be far too dangerous."

"You are a very thoughtful hippo, Hilmy," said Mina. "You could have tried to rescue the poor little monkey to show everyone how brave you are. But you have thought only of the little monkey's safety. You are a very kind hippo, Hilmy."

At that moment a large eagle swooped down and plucked the little monkey from the branches. The eagle gently dropped the monkey on the ground and then swooped up into the sky and flew away.

Everyone cheered. *"Subhan Allah,"* they called. The little monkey was now safe.

Hilmy hung his head in shame. He turned to Mina, Bill Hornbill and the jackal and said: "I am so ashamed of myself. I have lied to you all. I cannot fly, I cannot run as fast as the cheetah nor can I climb trees or scramble up cliffs. I so much wanted new friends and thought that was the way to find them. *Astaghfirullah*, I was wrong. I know that friendship is built on truth. We must never lie. I am truly sorry."

"Since you have now told us the truth Hilmy," replied Mina, "you can be my friend."

"Yes," said Bill Hornbill, "I will be your friend, Hilmy, provided you never lie again."

The jackal looked at Hilmy and said kindly: "It takes courage to admit that you have been lying. *Masha' Allah*, I am proud of you Hilmy for telling us the truth. Allah has taught us that it is wrong to lie. When we lie we will always be found out."

Hilmy returned to his waterhole. The water shone brightly beneath the bright blue sky. The little blue dragonfly called from a water lily leaf: "Welcome home Hilmy."

"*Al-Hamdulillah*, I have made some new friends," shouted Hilmy as he splashed into the water. He popped his head above the surface and said to the blue dragonfly: "I have learned that you do not have to lie to make friends. True friends judge you on who you really are, and not what you can do."

"That is a valuable lesson Hilmy, one we can all learn," smiled the blue dragonfly.

"Yes," said Hilmy thoughtfully. "Lies get us into trouble, not out of it. *Astaghfirullah*, I will never lie again."

GLOSSARY
of Islamic Terms

As-Salamu 'Alaykum
Literally "Peace be upon you", the traditional Muslim greeting, offered when Muslims meet each other.

Wa 'Alaykum as-Salam
"Peace be upon you too", is the reply to the greeting, expressing their mutual love, sincerity and best wishes.

Insha' Allah
Literally "If Allah so wishes". Used by Muslims to indicate their decision to do something, provided they get help from Allah. It is recommended that whenever Muslims resolve to do something and make a promise, they should add "Insha' Allah".

Fi Amanillah
Literally "In the safe custody of Allah". Used on the occasion of saying farewell to someone.

Subhan Allah
Literally "Glory be to Allah". It reflects a Muslim's appreciation and amazement at observing any manifestation of Allah's greatness.

Masha' Allah
Literally "As Allah may wish". Used on happy occasions, reflecting a Muslim's total surrender to Divine will.

Astaghfirullah
Literally "I seek pardon and forgiveness from Allah". Used to ward off an evil thought or to express regret over a bad action.

Al-Hamdulillah
Literally "Praise be to Allah". It is used for expressing thanks and gratefulness to Allah. This supplication is also used when one sneezes, in order to thank Allah.

Some information about
the Animals and Insects

Hornbill
Hornbills are birds, which live in tropical and sub-tropical areas of the world. They are named after their large downward curved bill. They eat insects and fruit.

Cheetah
The cheetah is a member of the cat family. It is the fastest animal on earth. It can be distinguished from other large cats by the 'tear marks' on the face. They are carnivorous and hunt during the day.

Jackal
The jackal is a member of the dog family. They are active both at night and during the day. Jackals are carnivorous; they hunt and scavenge.

Giraffe
The giraffe is the tallest animal on earth. They are often found in herds of 12-15 giraffes. Both male and female have short horns. Giraffes are vegetarians but they only eat leaves and not grass.

Eagle
Eagles are raptors, i.e. birds of prey. They have powerful feet called talons and a short, curved beak. They eat reptiles and small mammals. Some eagles eat fish.